Sniffy and Suzy

Sniffy said to Suzy, his friend,

Beneath a tree one day,

"Say, do you think that God intends

To send a flood our way?

Our friends are coming from the plains,

Some from the hills, no doubt.

They're lining up so when it rains,

They'll be inside, not out."

The monkeys did as they were told,

Giraffes and lions, too.

The elephants, who were so bold,

And both the kangaroos.

The camels trotted down the slope,

To the hippopotamus,

Then came the deer and antelope,

And the rhinoceros.

"They're on the deck and some below,

And we should go, I think."

But Suzy said, "We can't go,

They'd say that we both stink."

"Suzy, God called us from the dark,

And though we don't know why,

He told us to go into the Ark,

Be saved and multiply."

"I don't know why He'd include us,

But now we must obey.

God is in charge, no need to fuss,

I'm sure we'll be okay.

Let's go ahead and trust our Lord,

No matter what others say.

As Noah and his family board,

We, too, will make our way."

The folks outside did not believe.

They laughed, but soon would cry.

God said a flood they would receive,

And God would never lie.

"Suzy, we're safe inside this boat.

Look, dark clouds fill the sky.

It won't be long until we float,

As waters rise so high."

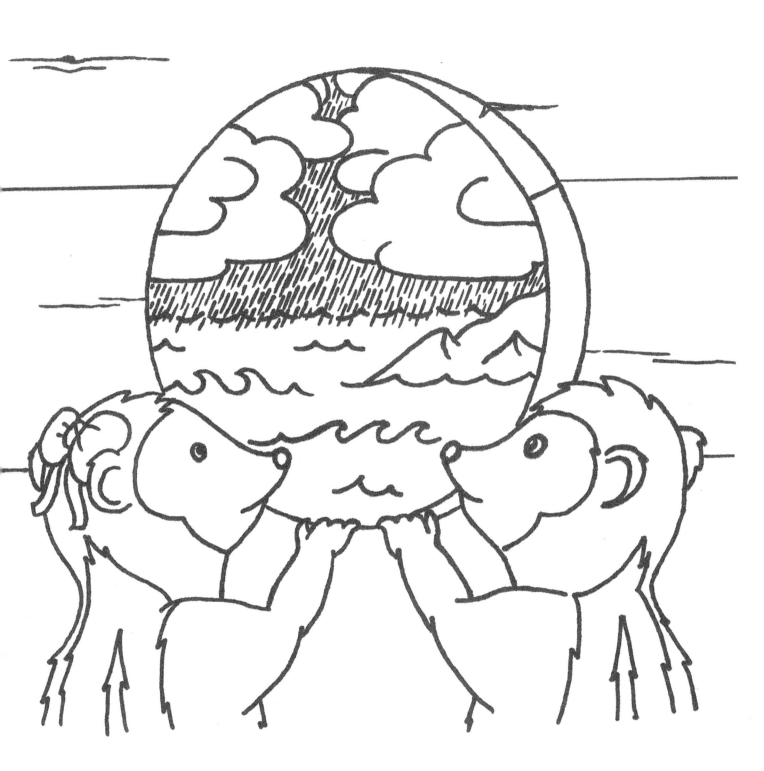

"I'm so glad we obeyed God's words

And on Him we did rely.

Just like our friends and little birds,

He kept us safe and dry."

CPSIA information can be obtained at www.ICGtesting.com
Printed in the USA
LVOW05s1513270315

432100LV00002B/9/P